© 1993 Geddes & Grosset Ltd
Reprinted 1994
Published by Geddes & Grosset Ltd,
New Lanark, Scotland.

ISBN 1 85534 566 8

Printed and bound in Slovenia.

The Ugly Duckling

Retold by Judy Hamilton
Illustrated by R. James Binnie

Tarantula Books

It was a sunny day in spring, and the river sparkled as it danced past the farmyard. A little boy saw a solitary egg lying in the rushes.

"What are you doing here?" he said. "You should be snug and warm under your mother's feathers!"

He carefully picked up the egg, and took it over to the duck's nest hidden behind the barn. The mother duck had left the nest for a moment. The boy put the egg in the nest. It was bigger than the other eggs. "You're going to be a prize duck!" he said to it. The mother duck returned to her nest and was a little puzzled to see five eggs.

"I'm sure I only laid four!" she muttered. "But never mind. They are all my babies!"

She settled herself on the eggs, and waited…

Days passed and at last the patience of the mother duck was rewarded. One by one, the eggs cracked open and the baby birds struggled out. The mother duck stood back to count and admire her babies. "One—oh how sweet!" she quacked. "Two—so fluffy! Three—oh, he's got his father's good looks. Four—a duckling to be proud of! Five—…"

The mother duck paused. Number five was not a very pretty duckling.

"Five—," the mother duck continued, trying not show her disappointment, "a duckling who will grow to be beautiful, I am sure!" After all, he was her baby and she loved him.

Trying not to worry, the mother duck waddled down to the river to get something tasty for her babies to eat.

The mother duck fussed over her ducklings, and they loved her dearly in return, following her everywhere. She taught them to swim, and how to dive down in the river to feed. She paraded proudly through the farmyard with them in a neat little line behind her. If she was a little sad that one of her babies was not as pretty as all the rest, she certainly never showed it. She loved him just as much as the others. What did upset her was the way that the other birds and animals laughed at him. They called him the Ugly Duckling, and would tease him constantly.

"Call yourself a duckling?" they jeered, "You're as scruffy as a scarecrow's hat!" The poor little fellow ran to his mother for comfort.

Soon the time came when the ducklings became old enough to mix with the other ducks around the farm. Without his mother to protect him the ugly duckling was teased and bullied more than he could bear. Even his own brothers and sisters turned on him.

"You're so ugly!" they said. "Stay away from us!"

Then they would peck him and flap their wings. The ugly duckling had to run away and hide.

Finally the day came when he could put up with it no more. The farm cat had scratched him. The geese had chased him away. His brothers and sisters had gone for a swim on the river and left him alone. Nobody except his mother liked him or wanted him. Sadly, the ugly duckling waddled away from the farm yard.

The ugly duckling had never been far from the farm before. The world outside was frightening. Autumn leaves were falling from the trees. The wind howled down the river valley and ruffled his stubbly feathers. It became dark and the shadows danced around him menacingly. Poor little ugly duckling. He hid himself in a clump of bushes and waited for daylight. When morning came, he carried on his lonely way. He waddled on for days and days, not knowing where he was going.

The days grew colder and colder. Winter was coming, and the ugly duckling knew he would have to find somewhere sheltered to spend the winter. At last, one day he came upon a small lake surrounded by rushes. This was just the place.

For the first few weeks the ugly duckling was quite content in his winter home. The rushes gave him shelter from the icy wind and there was plenty food in the lake. But it was to be a very bad winter that year. The weather became colder and colder. Soon, ice began to form on the lake, and the duckling had to swim in and out of the patches of ice to find food. Then, one day, he woke to find that the lake was completely frozen over. He skidded and slipped all over the surface trying to find a place where the ice was thin enough to break, but in vain. He hammered the surface with his beak but he could not get through to the water underneath to feed.

Wearily, he slithered back to the shelter of the rushes, hungry and cold.

Days passed. The snow lay thick on the ground.

The ugly duckling grew weaker. He was too weak even to try to find food. He lay in the rushes, cold, tired and sick.

He would probably have died, had nobody found him, but one day a man out walking with his dog came to his rescue. The dog noticed the ugly duckling first. Snuffling through the rushes it caught the smell of bird and began to bark. The man came to see why the dog was barking just as it found the ugly duckling. The ugly duckling was too weak even to feel afraid of the dog.

The man pushed the dog aside, and seeing the poor little half-dead bird, he picked him up and took him home.

For a few days the ugly duckling was treated with kindness such as he had never known since he left his mother's protection. In a cosy box by the stove he rested and warmed himself. The man and his wife fed him first of all with milk and water from dropper, then, when he was stronger, with bread and warm milk from a saucer. When they spoke to him their voices were gentle and kind. Even the dog seemed to treat him with loving care. It would nuzzle the ugly duckling softly with its nose. Sometimes it would even give him a very gentle lick and settle down beside him to go to sleep.

The ugly duckling was happy for the first time in his life, and wanted to stay there forever, but this was not to be.

As the ugly duckling grew stronger and the weather turned a little milder, the kind man decide he was ready to go back outside.

"Come on little fellow," he said, "you can stay in our back yard. There's a nice warm outhouse for you to sleep in, and a stream nearby. Our hens will keep you company." But as soon as the man left him, the hens gathered round him, laughing and jeering. "What a scrawny neck! What untidy feathers! You are ugly!"

Then, some boys passing in the lane beside the yard saw him.

"Get the ugly bird!" they yelled, hurling stones a him. The ugly duckling knew he had no choice. A soon as he got the chance, he ran away again.

The ugly duckling found his way back to the lake and his hideaway in the rushes. Luckily, the rest of the winter was not so cold as before. The lake did have ice on it at times but did not freeze over completely again. The ugly duckling survived the rest of the winter, still hiding.

Finally, slowly, spring came. New buds appeared on the trees, soft rain instead of sleet fell on the lake and daffodils appeared in the fields nearby.

One bright day, the ugly duckling was swimming on the lake when a flock of swans flew overhead. "How graceful and beautiful they are!" he thought. "How I wish I looked like them." He gazed at the white birds until they were out of sight, then heaved a sigh and swam on his way.

The ugly duckling spent more and more time out on the water as the days grew longer and the weather grew warmer. He liked the cool water beneath him and the warm sunshine on his back. He was still very lonely, but he felt safer that way.

Then one day, the swans appeared again in the sky above him. The ugly duckling looked upwards. Suddenly, one of the birds spotted him and flew down, splashing into the water beside him. The others followed. The ugly duckling was terrified, but there was nowhere to hide.

To his surprise, however, the swans did not laugh at him. They were looking at him in admiration!

"What a fine young fellow you are," said one. "Why are you alone?"

The ugly duckling hung his head in shame. "Nobody likes me because I'm ugly," he muttered. "I'm just an ugly duckling!"

"Nonsense!" the swans cried. "Look at your reflection in the lake. You're a beautiful swan!"

Nervously, the ugly duckling looked down at the water and saw the head of a fine swan. "Is that *me*?" he asked.

The swans nodded. "You never were a duckling. You were a cygnet. And now you're a swan!"

The young swan stretched his long white neck and turned to admire his magnificent white wings.

"I'm a swan!" he gasped.

And as he flew off with his friends he was proud—very proud indeed.